The Snow Country Prince

written by **DAISAKU IKEDA**

illustrated by **BRIAN WILDSMITH**

English version by Geraldine McCaughrean

Alfred A. Knopf   New York

IN THE LAND called the Snow Country, the end of summer changes everything. The fishermen must beach their boats, turn their backs on the stormy sea, and travel inland to the cities to find other work.

Little Mariko and her brother, Kazuo, dreaded the coming of the cold. It stung their eyes and made their hearts shiver. Their father was a fisherman, and when the winter arrived, they knew he too had to leave and would be gone from home till spring.

As the first snows fell, Mariko and Kazuo and their mother and their grandmother waved good-bye. "Not long till spring!" Papa called. But the wind whisked his words away, and flying snowflakes soon hid him from sight.

High overhead, as white as the snow, the first swans were arriving. Each year they came to shelter among the rushes, where the sea crept ashore in long fingers of blue.

And behind them came the north wind, colder than even Grandmother could ever remember. It froze the fingers of water from blue to white, and the swans struggled to find food.

"We must feed them or they will die!" said Mariko. So every day the children sprinkled corn for the swans while the ice sheets grew and ground together and growled fiercely.

One night as the children lay in bed, a snow-bright face appeared suddenly at their bedroom window. There in a fold of blizzard, crowned and robed in a dazzle of frost-glory, stood a young man. "I am the Snow Country Prince, guardian of the birds! When ice is sharp and drifts are deep, I ride on the wind to watch over my subjects. Never have I known such a cruel winter!

"Though I came as fast as I could, I feared that many swans had died on the frozen fringes of the sea. But what do I find? All well, because of the kindness of Mariko and Kazuo! I thank you! And I tell you this in return: *Whatever happens, don't give up.*" Then a kite tail of wind carried the Snow Prince away across the sky.

After that visit, no trouble or kindness was too much for Kazuo and
Mariko. They fed the swans every day. And when they found one left torn
and bleeding on the ice by cruel wolves, they carried it home to the village
—to a warm shed and a soft bed. They were sure the Snow Country Prince
would want them to care for the swan.

"The swan mustn't die!" declared Kazuo. "How would the Snow Country Prince feel? We mustn't fail him."

The people in the village were amazed to see how tenderly the children cared for that poor, sick bird. "You never give up, do you?" said the old man next door, and smiled. In fact, wherever the children went, it seemed that people's faces broke into a smile...

Until the letter came that made their mother cry.

"Papa has had an accident," she told them, drying her eyes. "I must go to him."

The sleigh took them all to the railway station, and Mariko and Kazuo now had to wave good-bye to their mother, as they had to Papa. The cold of loneliness bit into their hearts.

"Remember," said Grandmother, "Mama and Papa are lonely for you too."

Now every day—in addition to feeding the birds and nursing the sick swan—Mariko and Kazuo wrote to their father in the hospital. They drew pictures and described how, with their help, their patient got stronger... and fitter...and happier every day.

Mama pinned the pictures over Papa's bed. Just seeing them made him feel better. The more pictures there were, the better he felt. Stronger and fitter and happier…just like the swan!

The weather, too, got better day by day. The fingers of sea unfroze, turning from white to blue. The swans sheltering there prepared to fly away to their spring feeding grounds.

The children carried the injured swan and gently placed it in the water. It lifted its head hopefully toward the sky and flapped its wings.

"Yes, you can do it too! You *can*!" cried Mariko encouragingly. "Keep trying! Don't give up!"

"No, whatever happens, *don't give up*!" said Kazuo. The words seemed to have been waiting in his heart.

And the wind seemed to sigh the very same thing.

One evening, the sky overhead filled with swans. Each as white as snow, each as beautiful as the Snow Country Prince himself, they hurtled one by one into the sky until only a single shining swan remained.

"You can do it! You can go too!" called Mariko and Kazuo to the swan they had nursed.

With its feathers touched by the gold of the setting sun and with a gust of
wind beneath its wings, the swan rose into the air to follow the rest.

Then suddenly the tears came. "First Papa...then Mama...and now even our swan has gone away!" said Mariko. "Oh, how lonely winter is!"

But winter was over.

Warmth came back to the Snow Country.

And so did Mama.

And so did Papa—as well and as strong and as happy as any soaring swan on the wing.

So too did the Snow Country Prince, though the children mistook his spring robes for blossoms and his words for the soft spring wind when he whispered,

"Well done, Mariko, my Snow Princess!
Well done, Kazuo, my Princeling of
the Snow Country!"

THIS IS A BORZOI BOOK PUBLISHED BY ALFRED A. KNOPF, INC.

Text Copyright © 1990 by Daisaku Ikeda
English version Copyright © 1990 by Geraldine McCaughrean
Illustrations Copyright © 1990 by Brian Wildsmith
All rights reserved under International and Pan-American Copyright Conventions. Published in
the United States by Alfred A. Knopf, Inc., New York. Distributed by Random House, Inc.,
New York. Originally published by Oxford University Press in 1990.
Manufactured in Hong Kong 1 2 3 4 5 6 7 8 9 10

Library of Congress Cataloging-in-Publication Data
Ikeda, Daisaku. [Yukiguni no ōjisama. English]
The Snow Country Prince / written by Daisaku Ikeda ; illustrated by Brian Wildsmith.
p.   cm. Translation of: Yukiguni no ōjisama.
Summary: Encouraged by the words of the Snow Country Prince, Mariko and Kazuo nurse an
injured swan back to health during the long winter.
ISBN 0-679-81965-7 (trade)   ISBN 0-679-91965-1 (lib. bdg.)
[1. Folklore—Japan.] I. Wildsmith, Brian, ill. II. Title. PZ8.1.I34Sn 1991
398.22'0952—dc20   90-24908

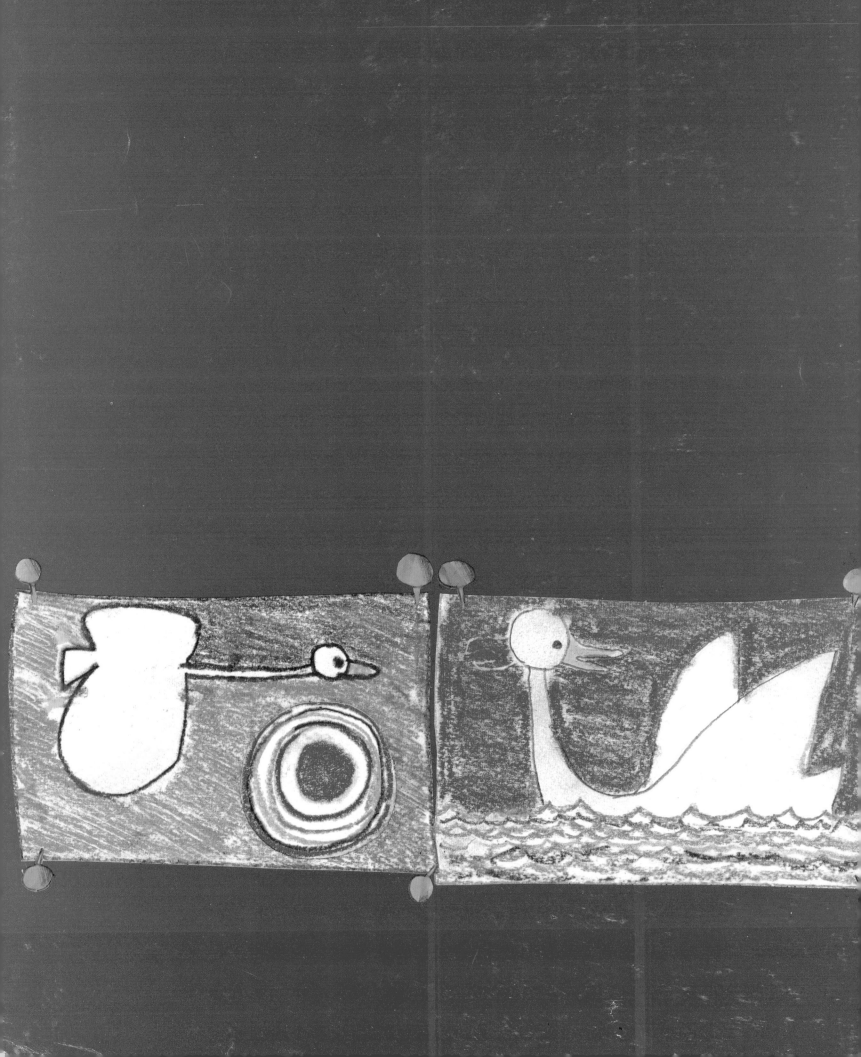